# TWO *is a* TEAM

## by *LORRAINE* and *JERROLD BEIM*

### PICTURES BY ERNEST CRICHLOW

*A Voyager Book*
NEW YORK
HARCOURT BRACE JOVANOVICH, INC.

Library of Congress Cataloging in Publication Data

Beim, Lorraine (Levey) 1909–1951.
Two is a team.

(A Voyager book, AVB 86)
SUMMARY: After disagreement in building a coaster,
a black boy and his white playmate learn the value of
working together on a project.
[1. Friendship—Fiction] I. Beim, Jerrold, 1910–
1957, joint author. II. Crichlow, Ernest T., date
illus. III. Title.
PZ7.B3883Tw10        [E]        73-12939

ISBN 0-15-692050-6

Printed in the United States of America

A B C D E F G H I J

# TWO *is a* TEAM

Ted and Paul were friends. They played together every day after school. "We're just the same age!" they told Ted's mother when they played at his house.

"And we're just the same size," they showed Paul's mother when they played at his house.

One afternoon they were playing on the street and saw some boys go whizzing by on their coasters. "I wish I had a coaster," Ted said. And then Paul had an idea. "Let's make one," he cried.

"I have an old roller skate we could use for the wheels," Ted said. "There's a box and some wood in my cellar," Paul said. They both ran home as fast as they could for the things to make the coaster.

When they came back Ted started to attach the roller skate wheels to a piece of wood. "That's not the way. Let me do it," Paul said. "I can do it myself!" Ted answered, and he wouldn't let Paul help him.

Paul took the hammer and started to nail the box to the piece of wood. "You're not doing it right," Ted said. "I am too!" Paul answered, and he wouldn't let Ted help him.

"Give me the hammer," Ted said. "I'm going to put the handle on." "No, you're not," Paul told him. "I'm going to do it." Paul tried to keep the hammer but Ted pulled it away from him.

"I'm not going to make a coaster with you." Paul pushed Ted. "Who wants to make one with you?" Ted shoved Paul. Paul took his box and piece of wood. Ted took his roller skate. They were so mad at each other they didn't even say good-bye.

When Ted got home, he started to make his own coaster. He found an old box and a piece of wood and made the coaster the way he wanted to.

When Paul got home he started to make his own coaster. He found some old baby carriage wheels and made the coaster the way he wanted to.

The boys met on the street the next day
with their new coasters. "My coaster's

better than yours," Paul said. "Mine's better than yours," Ted said. "Let's have a race and see!"

They took their coasters to the top of a hill. "Get ready—get set—go!" they called.

The race was on! Down—down the hill they went on their coasters—so fast they couldn't stop.

Down—down the hill they went—so fast they didn't see the lady crossing the street with her bundles. They almost bumped into her and her bundles went spilling to the ground.

Down—down the hill they went—so fast they didn't see the little girl crossing the street with her doll carriage. They bumped right into the carriage and the doll went tumbling to the ground.

Down—down the hill they went—so fast
they didn't see the man crossing the street
with his dog. They almost bumped into
him and the dog ran away.

Down—down the hill they went—and
when they almost reached the bottom—
what do you think happened?

"My wheels came off!" Ted cried. "My box came off!" Paul said. Then they looked up and they saw a man, a lady, and a little girl.

"You made me drop my bundles and a bottle of milk was broken," the lady said. "You bumped my carriage and broke my doll," the little girl said. "My dog ran away and when I got him he'd lost his leash," the man said. "You boys will have to pay for all you've done."

Poor Ted and Paul! They didn't know how they were going to pay for all they'd done. They started home together, looking sad and worried, carrying the parts of their coasters with them.

They were almost home when they saw
a sign in a grocery store window.

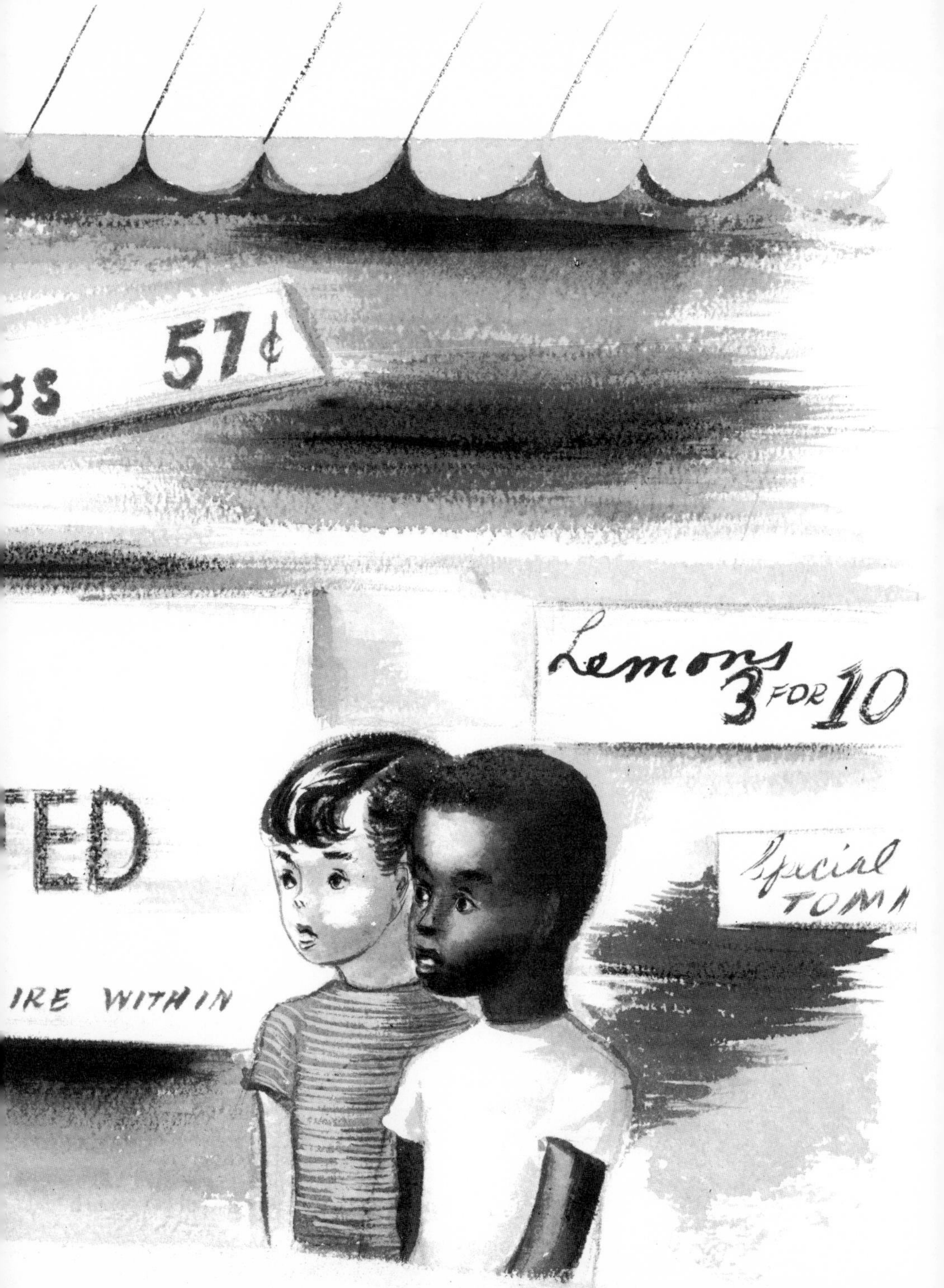
57¢
Lemons
3 FOR 10
ED
IRE WITHIN
Special
TOM

"Why don't we get a job?" Ted said. They went into the grocery store. "Could you use two delivery boys?" they asked. "Well, I could," the man behind the counter said, "but you have to have your own wagon to deliver the groceries."

"We haven't a wagon," Paul said. Then Ted had a wonderful idea. "We'll be back to work with a wagon tomorrow," he said. "A wagon! Where will we get a wagon?" Paul asked when they went out. "We'll make one," Ted answered. "Out of our coasters!"

And they did! They worked hard the rest of the day building a wagon. Paul let Ted help him put the box on. Ted let Paul help him put the wheels on. And together they made a fine strong wagon!

Every day after school they worked together. Sometimes Ted steered the wagon and Paul delivered the groceries. Sometimes Paul steered and Ted delivered the groceries.

They paid the lady back for her milk.

They paid the little girl back for her doll.

They paid the man back for his dog's leash.

And they learned how to drive their wagon down a hill—zig-zagging around anyone with bundles, carriages, or dogs. That was the most fun of all!